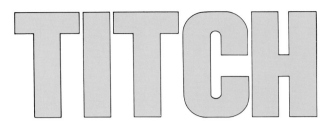

TITCH

TITCH

by PAT HUTCHINS

Red Fox

TITCH BOOKS BY PAT HUTCHINS IN RED FOX
Titch
Titch and Daisy
Tidy Titch
You'll Soon Grow into Them, Titch

A Red Fox Book

Published by Random House Children's Books
20 Vauxhall Bridge Road, London SW1V 2SA

A division of Random House UK Ltd
London Melbourne Sydney Auckland
Johannesburg and agencies throughout the world

Copyright © Pat Hutchins 1971

7 9 10 8 6

First published in the USA by
The Macmillan Company 1971

First published in Great Britain by
The Bodley Head 1972

Red Fox edition 1997

Printed in Singapore

RANDOM HOUSE UK Limited Reg. No. 954009

ISBN 0 09 926253 3

For Darren

Titch was little.

His sister Mary
was a bit bigger.

And his brother Pete
was a lot bigger.

Pete had a great big bike.

Mary had a big bike.

And Titch had a little tricycle.

Pete had a kite
that flew high
above the trees.

Mary had a kite
that flew high
above the houses.

And Titch had a pinwheel
that he held in his hand.

Pete had a big drum.

Mary had a trumpet.

And Titch had
a little wooden whistle.

Pete had a big saw.

Mary had a big hammer.

And Titch held the nails.

Pete had a big spade.

Mary had a fat flowerpot.

But Titch had the tiny seed.

And Titch's seed grew

and grew

and grew.